Josephine Hannon

Leo

A tale

Josephine Hannon

Leo
A tale

ISBN/EAN: 9783742857460

Manufactured in Europe, USA, Canada, Australia, Japa

Cover: Foto ©Andreas Hilbeck / pixelio.de

Manufactured and distributed by brebook publishing software
(www.brebook.com)

Josephine Hannon

Leo

LÉO

A Tale

BY

M. J. H.

—◁●▷—

DUBLIN

M. H. GILL AND SON

50 UPPER SACKVILLE STREET

1883

LEO.

CHAPTER I.

ALL the clocks in Helstone were striking six, at least such of them as kept time together; for it was a proverb in the old town that they all "agreed to differ."

It had been pouring rain all day long, and the weather had had a depressing effect on the inmates of the nursery and schoolroom at Lincroft Villa,—especially upon the third member of the family, whose baptismal name was Leonora, but whom everybody called "Leo" for short, and who was just seven years old.

But a more important event than a rainy day had taken place—an event which had anything but a soothing effect on the spirits of Miss Leo: her "nose was completely out of joint," because she had been forbidden to go near her mother's bedroom or to make the slightest noise.

"Bother that child!" she said, impatiently

stamping her little foot, as she turned away from
the window, where she had been tracing with her
finger the raindrops as they slowly trickled down the
window-pane.   "Bother that child!   I can't see
what it wants coming worrying here for."

"Bother *what* child, Leo?" asked her elder sister,
Edith, looking up from a bunch of cherries she was
painting.

"Why, that tiresome new baby, of course," answered Leo, indignantly.   "There, I can't go near
mamma, and I'm so full of trouble and anxiety about
Miss Rosa.   You mayn't believe me, Edie, but she's
been ill for the last month, and won't look at her
food, much less taste it."

(Here it may be mentioned that the young lady in
question was a large wax doll.)

"Why don't you take her on your lap and nurse
her?" suggested Edith; "you don't pet her enough,
you know.   I daresay she's only suffering from low
spirits, and people like that require a great deal of
coaxing and kissing to bring them round."

"Oh! I'm sick and tired of the old thing; she's
sick all over, from the crown of her head to the sole
of her foot, and she throws up bran, and I don't like
to clean up after her.   I don't know; I dont think,
after all, its Miss Rosa I am so anxious about; but
I *do* so want to go to mamma."

"You would not like to go and awake her, now that she's asleep, would you, dear?" said a young lady in mourning, who sat reading by the fire, and who was the children's governess.

"Oh! but, Miss Williams, it *is* so dull; I'm so sick and tired of doing nothing; and the rain makes me so cross, I can't get out.—Here, Trottie, I'll pelt you, if you don't come and play with me;" and forthwith she shied a large india-rubber ball at a little boy who was building a house of bricks in a corner of the room. One could tell by the way he handled the playthings, he was not quite like another child; he *felt* the toys more than he looked at them; —indeed, the latter he could not do, for poor little Trottie Mildmay was blind. His real name was Emmanuel Ernest, but it had been too long to adopt at first, and nobody remembered how or when the "Trottie" had originated. He was everybody's pet, and yet he was not the least bit spoiled, for his mother had always taught him God's will was best; and so the little fellow accepted sweetly the affliction which Jesus, whom he loved so much, had sent him.

Leo was the plague of his life, but he took her rough ways as he took his blindness, as sent by his Heavenly Father; and though they were twins, he acted to her more like an elder brother than a child of her own age. Patient he always was with her;

but there was something more in the way he pro-
tected her, as far as it lay in his feeble power—in
the way, too, in which he soothed her when she
cried, more often from temper, it is to be feared,
than for sorrow.

But to all this love Leo paid little heed; she took
it as her due, and seldom thought of thanking the
patient little brother for all his sweetness to her.

Even now, as he felt the ball shattering his care-
fully-built house, he did not start up in anger with
her, but turned his beautiful sightless eyes to where
he guessed Leo was standing, and asked quietly,
"what she would like to do?"

"Why play, of course, silly!" cried Leo. "Come,
let's have a gallop round the room, or hide-and-go-
seek, or something."

Now, if there was one thing Trottie hated, it was
a noisy romping game, such as Leo loved; and this
was only natural, poor little fellow, since he could
only *feel* where he was going. But he did not com-
plain now; so gathering his bricks together, he
carefully put them away in his toy cupbord, and
then was ready to do Leo's pleasure.

By the time he had finished, however, Leo had
altered her mind. Her maternal affections had been
aroused by hearing, as she thought, one of her dolls
crying out for her; and in a remorseful spirit, she

declared her intention of giving them a tea-party to make up for her neglect. She requested Miss Williams to write "very big" on a sheet of paper: "All contributions thankfully received," as she had heard people did when they begged for some charity; and then added, "for the doll's tea-party." But as this was not successful, she was forced to slip out to the kitchen, and try her coaxing powers on the cook. But cook required very little of Miss Leo's "blarney," as she called it, and willingly filled the widespread pinafore with sweets and cakes.

"Now a grain o' tay, cook," coaxed the wee fairy, imitating to perfection the brogue of the good-natured servant; "an' a pinch o' sugar, an' a dhrop o' milk."

"Musha, alana, an' is it thryin' to mimic me ye are? Thin it's yerself is the finest little lady goin', Miss Leo."

She restrained her joy until past her mother's bedroom door; but once crossed the threshold of the schoolroom, her delight found vent in a series of shouts, which thrilled through the delicate frame of poor little Trottie.

"Oh! look, Trot! look, and look, and look!" she cried, depositing her treasures, one by one, on the floor. "Come along, and let's have a real jolly feast."

Everybody said that Leo ought to have been a boy, and Trottie a girl, their characters were so utterly opposite, and seemed so unsuited to the sex to which they respectively belonged.

Even now, as they arranged the doll's tea-party, it could be seen that Trottie knew a good deal more about it than his sister; his sensitive power of touch made him lay a thing just in its right place, while Leo dashed cups and saucers right, left, and centre, not knowing in the least how to make it bright for her poor children, the dollies.

"Leo, you've forgotten to send out invitations," remonstrated Trottie; "and it's awfully rude to give such short notice before a tea-party; you know the poor ladies haven't time to get their grand dresses ready,"

"No more we have," said Leo, penitently. "Well, at all events, it's too late now, and they are all old friends, and so won't mind. Then, too, I'm *sure* they don't know it's the fashion."

"'Where ignorance is bliss, 'tis folly to be wise,'" quoted Edith, busy still with her cherries.

"What does that mean, Edith?" asked Trottie.

"Oh! you'll know some day, dear little man," returned his sister; "you're quite too little to understand it now."

"Ah! don't bother about Edie's nonsense; she's

always saying poetry," exclaimed Leo, impatiently twitching Trottie by the sleeve. " Come on, let's say grace and begin. You're to be papa, you know, and I'll be mamma. Mamma, that is, *our* mamma, you know, is to be grandmamma, who is very ill, and cannot come downstairs. Papa is grandpapa——"

" And what am I to be ?" asked Edith.

" Oh ! you'll do for an aunt, like Aunt Cattie, you know ; and Father Cogan will be himself—we ought to have asked him to our party ; it doesn't do not to have a priest ;—never mind, though, we'll ask him next time. Now, let's begin. Oh ! I forgot to say, Rosa and Violet are our only children, except a big son, who is away at sea, like Arthur " (Arthur was Leo's big brother), " and all the rest of the dolls are company. Now, let's begin in real earnest. *I'm* going to imitate Mrs. Clincher, and let you be like Mr. Clincher.

" Rosa, my sweet child, you're not behaving as polite as I'd like to the dear little girl beside you ; hand her some cake before helping yourself, my darling."

Then she went on, aside to Trottie :

" My dear, Rosa's health is failing fast ; she spits bran like anything. You really must fetch a doctor."

" Very well dear ; I'll do as you say," returned her obedient husband.

"My dear, I wish you'd take more notice of our sweet children," she whined; "they're really lovely creatures—quite unlike other people's; and yet you never take the smallest notice of them. Here, nurse Violet a bit," and she flopped a big wax doll into her little brother's arms.

"Children," said a voice they all knew to be papa's, even before his head appeared in the doorway, "children, who cares to come for a little visit to mamma? She says it's a long time since she's seen you all, and she would like you to sit with her a bit to-night. But mind, Leo, no noise; you promise me this, don't you, dear?"

"Oh, yes, I promise anything—everything," cried the excited child; "and shall we see the new baby?"

"Yes, if you're good—" but Mr. Mildmay spoke to the air, for Leo had taken flight even before her own sentence was finished; and when the rest of the family reached the sick-room, they were not surprised to see her cosily nestling to the mother she had not seen for four days, with her curly, golden head pillowed on her shoulder.

"How are you, mother dear?" asked Edith, stooping down to kiss Mrs. Mildmay.

"Oh, much better and stronger to-night, my child. But where's Miss Williams; why didn't you bring her with you?" asked the invalid, always thoughtful for others.

"Here I am, Mrs. Mildmay," answered the governess. "I do hope you'll soon be strong enough to come downstairs."

"I hope the children have been very good, have they?" asked Mrs. Mildmay, glancing doubtfully at the head on her shoulder.

"Very good, indeed, I am glad to say," was the reply.

"And Leo?"

"Wonderful for her; really she's been a model of self-restraint and quietness since your illness, Mrs. Mildmay."

"How glad that makes me, my darling; it gives me new strength;" and the mother dropped a light kiss on the head beside her.

Leo shivered with very happiness: her love for her mother was her sheet anchor;—"for mamma" she would try to do anything. And was it any wonder, when such a wise, tender mother was hers?

"Come here, Trot," said Leo graciously from her snuggery; "why don't you go to mamma's other shoulder?"

"I'd tire her if I came Leo, so to-morrow will be my turn, won't it, mother?

"Yes, mannie, surely you shall come—now if you choose;" but, even as she said it, Miss Williams detected her endeavour to check a sigh of weariness,

and so marshalled her troop back to their own
quarters.

Mother's heart, however, yearned for a word from
her sightless treasure, and she detained him behind
the others.

"And how has it gone with my precious?" she
said, as the little head sank contentedly on her
shoulder.

"Oh, I was very lonely without you, mamma,"
he answered; "how glad I am that Jesus and the
Blessed Virgin are never ill, and we can't go to them.
All this time, which would have made me *so* tired,
I've felt them close to me, helping me, oh, ever, ever
so much to be good."

"Then you *have* been trying, my darling?"

"Oh, yes, mother; and the voices, you know, that
I wait and listen for have sounded sweeter and
sweeter."

"But don't you try, Trottie dear, not to dream
and think so much?" questioned Mrs. Mildmay,
anxiously, fearing that this waiting and listening,
as he called it, might only be the fruit of his
imagination.

"Yes, mamma," he said; "the voices come still,
even though I do my best not to think of them,
because you told me to try not to, though they
get seldomer and seldomer now, and yet sweeter and

sweeter. It's not quite *words* they say, but it sounds like when you play the piano gently in the dark, only far sweeter and softer; and the Blessed Virgin seems so near me then; 'specially if I've been trying very hard to be good and patient. I can only *feel* her near; but that is not strange, mother, is it, since I have no sight?"

There was no shade of sadness in the child's voice as he uttered those last words; how could he regret a loss he had never known? Rather did their simple faith strike Mrs. Mildmay as being very beautiful. This " waiting and listening " had been a favourite occupation with Trottie almost since he could speak. He used to say he heard the angels calling him; and that smote his mother's heart with pain, for she feared he might be taken from her as a little child. But later on he used to say it was his heavenly Mother come to comfort her child, for he had a strong and firm devotion to the Blessed Virgin.

He had been lying a few minutes quite quietly, only holding that converse with his mother that, perhaps, silence expresses more fully than any words, when he started up, listening intently.

" What is it, Trottie dear? " said Mrs. Mildmay.

A prolonged howl from schoolroomwards answered her; and in another instant, Leo, heedless of all injunctions burst into the room in floods of tears.

"Oh, mamma, mamma," she sobbed, " Miss Rosa's fainted! When papa called us to go to you, I was *so* glad, that I turned her over, and there she's been lying ever since! Oh, mamma, mamma, what *shall* I do? Give me some of that sal, sal, sal—what is it?—perhaps that will bring her to. Oh, my sweet Rosa, what a cruel mother I've been to you!"

Much relieved to find the situation no worse, Mrs. Mildmay asked to see the unfortunate doll.

"I left her there, and flew off to you, mamma; but I'll fetch her in a second." And in a second she reappeared with her baby. There was not much the matter with her really; only an ancient wound had begun to bleed bran, and the head had got an additional dent.

Soothed and comforted, after a great deal of pains, her contrite young mother was at last got off to bed, and so poor Trottie had to forego the pleasant chat with mother.

Patient little man! your turn will come to-morrow; and in the meantime say your say to the heavenly Mother, who can never weary or be ill.

CHAPTER II.

T was not long before Mrs. Mildmay was strong enough to come down stairs—and a joyful day her coming among them was to the children. Leo fairly pranced with delight, and Trottie, though not so boisterous, was quite as glad in his own way. It was easy to see the mother was enthroned in the hearts of her children; and she deserved so to be, for a greater, tenderer heart rarely watched over little ones.

It was agreed the event should be celebrated by a large children's party : and for this, invitations, according to Trottie's polite ritual, had been duly sent out. Leo, of course, was to be hostess, and Trottie host; the party was to be entirely the children's own ; at it they were to do as they liked, so long as they kept within the bounds of reason : and that was why Trottie kept coming anxiously to the nursery door, entreating Leo to make haste or he should have to receive the guests alone.

"Which shall it be, darling ?" said Mrs. Mildmay,

2

holding up two pretty dresses—one worn many times before, but fresh and pretty still, pretty in Leo's eyes because it had low neck and short sleeves; while the other, a new silk, with white muslin overall, was eyed anything but favourably, because it lacked these desideratums. At last the dotted muslin was decided on, and Leo appeared just as the first carriage-full entered the door.

There was great kissing and hand-shaking; for the Mildmays were general favourites in Helstone; especially Trottie, who made friends everywhere with his gentle, loving ways.

As the door closed upon the last of her expected little friends, Leo turned joyfully to the drawing-room, whither Trottie had already made his escape.— And a dear little hostess she made, that gay little chatterbox, with her golden curly head, large gray eyes, and laughing, saucy mouth. Most of the hard work of the entertainment fell upon *her* shoulders, for Trottie's affliction prevented his being of much use. Only now and then might he be seen talking to some little girl more shy, and, consequently, more lonely than the rest.

As soon as tea was over dancing, as a matter of course, was proposed, and Leo opened the quadrille with Harry Hill, her favourite of the moment. She would not hear of excusing her poor little brother;

so Alice Huntley, just such another character as himself, only a good deal older, led him gently and tenderly through his ordeal.

After a little, however, the queen of the revels pronounced dancing a "bore;" but mamma would not allow it to be done away with until she had the consent of all her little friends. They were only too delighted to change it to play; and "games, games," were voted for in all the keys of the gamut.

"Musical chairs" succeeded "Blind-man's Buff;" and it made everybody laugh to see how suddenly mamma stopped playing the piano, "just when they least expected it," they said. Then came "Hunt the Slipper," "Oranges and Lemons," and "Forfeits;" and as this last game was at its height, Mrs. Mildmay crossed to where Leo was standing, with sparkling eyes and on the very tiptoe of expectation, near Edith, who was giving out the articles to be reclaimed.

"Leo, darling, grandmamma wants to speak to you; she says you've not been near her the whole evening;—and that's not very kind, is it, little woman, when she's going away to-morrow?" said her mother.

"Oh, but I'm going with her," replied Leo, looking up confidently in Mrs. Mildmay's face.

This was the first *she* had heard of it; but as Leo had a trick of giving out her mind rather suddenly, she was not surprised at her now. However, she led off the rather unwilling young lady to talk to " grannie."

" Well, grannie, what do you want ?" began Leo, more impatiently than respectfully.

" Only to tell mamma about our plan for to-morrow, and to see if she approves of it, birdie," said the old lady, laying her withered cheek against the bright rosy one of her favourite grandchild.

At this the expression of Leo's face changed, and she became very grave. She had told her mother she was going home to-morrow with Mrs. Archer, but she had no more intention of doing so than the man in the moon. True, grannie had said she should like to take her home with her, but she had said the same scores of times before, and so she thought no more about it now than she had done then.

" Grandmamma," she said, " I'm afraid I can't go ; what would my Trottie do without me, and my babies. Miss Rosa is very poorly just now; ' in a fit of galloping consumption,' nurse says ; and what would mamma do without me to run her messages ? You see I should lose threepence a week. No, grannie, I think you must let me off."

" But," said the old lady, smiling at this quaint speech, which savoured strongly of the proverb, " one for Trottie and mamma, and two for myself ;" " if you like, Trottie shall come with you, though what I shall do with him I don't know," she continued. "I don't mean to hurt you, Edith, but I could never understand the child," she said, seeing the pained expression of her daughter's face; "however, if Leo likes, he shall come. Well, there's objection number one settled."

"Thanks, mamma; but I don't think I could part with Trottie," said Mrs. Mildmay.

"And *can* you part with Leo?" said that young lady, looking at her mother half-resentfully, half-lovingly.

"Not at all, darling," said Mrs. Mildmay, kissing her; "only, you know, Trot cannot see and *you* can, and this makes him more dependent on mother's love and care than you, don't you understand?"

"Yes, mamma; and I'm sorry I was selfish and unkind; I'll try and do without Trottie," she said, penitently, while the little mouth was put up for a kiss of forgiveness; "and, grandmamma, I'll bring Miss Rosa instead; for really, poor dear, she's in a pre— pre— ; what is that word, mamma?"

"Precarious?"

"Yes; in a very precarious state of health. But, then, what shall I do for my threepence a week?" and she looked doubtful.

"Oh, *I'll* give you sixpence, birdie," said her grandmother.

" Will that be quite prudent, mamma ?" questioned Mrs. Mildmay.

" Oh, yes ; it will only be for a few weeks, Edith," she returned, hastily ; " so let her be happy while she may."

" Well, run away now, dear," said Leo's mother ; " you must not forget your little guests : see, it's *your* turn now to reclaim your forfeit !"

She ended as Edith answered, " Leo Mildmay," to the task ; " she must put one hand where the other cannot reach it."

" Oh, but I can't do *that*," exclaimed Leo, turning for assistance to Mrs. Mildmay.

" And I'm afraid *I* can't help you," was the not encouraging reply. " Run and coax Edie ; I'm sure she can !"

But Trottie had come over to Leo, and was whispering to her earnestly ; and almost before Mrs. Mildmay had done, she placed her right hand under her left elbow, while her large eyes beamed with triumph.

But the first nurse had come for her charges now, and one by one they dropped off until none but the little host and hostess remained ; and it was not difficult to get them to bed to-night, for they were tired with the evening's pleasure and excitement.

Next morning Trottie felt himself rather roughly shaken out of a sweet sleep. It was Leo, of course, who stood in her snowy night-dress beside his cot, entreating of him to wake up and listen to a "wonderful lovely dream" she had had the night before.

"Listen, Trot," she cried excitedly, as she seated herself on a tiny chair and clasped one knee. "I thought I was in heaven, sitting on a pillar, only it was *so* queer I could not see the top of the pillar, and I thought I was crying, and then an angel that was *so* bright, so bright, that I could scarcely look at him, came to me and said: 'What are you crying for, little girl?' and I said it was because all those people—there were heaps, and lots, and crowds of them there—had beautiful white dresses and gold crowns and harps, and were singing, oh! ever so sweetly, and I wanted to be like them; and when I looked at myself, I was all dirty and raggedy; and then the beautiful angel said to me—let me see, I forget what he said, but it was something *very* nice;— but anyhow he took me into a big room where there were long tables, with, oh! such beautiful lots of white dresses on them, some big, some little, just to fit you and me, Trot; and then somehow we were in another room just as big, only *crowns* were on the tables, and I remember he said, 'Do you think you deserve one of these?' and I said, 'I didn't know,' and so he took one with one stone shining, like mamma's ring, in it and put it on my head; and when we went back

into the great big room, you know, where I was on
the pillar, I saw the other people had ever so many
stars in *their* crowns, and so I said to the angel: 'And
why have you only given *me* a crown with one?' and
then he said: 'Oh, but these people have done a good
thing for each one of those shining stars; and how
many have you done?' So I said I could not remember any, and then he said: 'Yes, *I* remember
one,' and so just then I awoke thinking—oh, I don't
know what, but ever so happy to have been in heaven;
and I'm quite sure I'll try and be *very* good, and get
lots of stars in my crown when I do really get to
heaven;—won't you, Trottie?" and the mobile face
looked unusually earnest and grave.

" Yes, Leo," was the ready answer. "Shall we ask
Holy Mary now, straight away, to help us?" and the
two tiny white-robed figures knelt down while Trottie
said the prayer.

But nurse soon came to dress them; and when
they went down stairs hand-in-hand, they found that
mother and grandmamma had talked over Leo's visit
to the Grange, and decided on her going. Only half
willingly had Mrs. Mildmay given her consent, for
she feared Mrs. Archer's indulgent training for her
wayward Leo; but then, she thought, "mamma is
aged and delicate, and does not often see the children, and it would be hard to deny her this little

request that she seems to have so set her heart on. So she said "Yes," praying earnestly, meanwhile, that Jesus and Mary would watch over her little girl, and not let her be spoiled in the short time she hoped she would be away.

So it was settled Leo should go home with grand-mamma for three whole weeks, during which time Trottie was to write to her *every day* (the poor little man could not hold a pen yet); he was to take a mother's care of her children, the dolls, and on no account to break *one* of her playthings. Edith was to make a pink silk dress for Miss Rosa against her return. Miss Williams was to pray with all her might and main that ' she might be a good child, not tease grandmamma, and not come home in dis-grace. Mamma was to watch over Trottie and not tease him *too* much, only just a little to keep him in practice. And papa was to be sure not to forget to come fetch her just exactly that day three weeks, to the very hour and minute.

These injunctions given, she heaved a sigh of re-lief, and set off pretty contented at grandmamma's side, waving her handkerchief and kissing her hands as hard as she could.

" They had to travel far that day; and the novelty of being in the train for a time took up all Leo's thoughts; but grandmamma having fallen asleep,

Leo, who was used to much attention, soon woke her up exclaiming: "Grannie, grannie, I never knew God pump so hard before, did you?"

"Never knew God *pump* so hard before," repeated Mrs. Archer ; "what on earth do you mean, Leo?"

"Why, what I say, grannie," she answered, rather pertly; but her grandmother was far too foolishly fond of her to correct her; "don't you know that when it rains, God is pumping up in heaven?"

"Whoever put such an idea as that into your head, child," said the old lady,' "it's quite silly and ridiculous!"

"I put it into my own head, grannie, for nobody ever told me of it; and it's not a bit *ridikilis*, if you think a bit. When Sarah, the cook at home, puts the handle of the pump up and down, so," and she imitated the movement, "she brings up water; and when God does just the same with a great big pump He has up in heaven, rain falls down into the world ; dòn't you see, grannie, it's quite simple."

"Quite simple, yes," returned her grandmother, sleepily, and she closed her eyes again, too weary to explain how the rain fell, and what it was, to her little grandchild.

Then Leo fell asleep also, and did not wake until the stars were shining high and bright in the deep blue sky. By this time grandmamma was thoroughly

awake too, and Leo began telling her her theory of
the stars.

"Grandmamma, aren't the stars very beautiful
little things?" she said.

"Yes, my darling," answered the old lady; "do
you know that poem 'Twinkle, twinkle, little star?'"

"Of course I do," cried the child. "Why I knew
it *years* ago!"

Mrs. Archer smiled at this assertion of the few-
year-old Leo.

"But, grandmamma, what do *you* think the stars
are?"

"I don't know, I'm sure, my child," said her
grandmother, a little tired of Leo's theories.

"Shall I tell you what *I* think they are, grandmamma?"

"Yes, my dear," she replied, feeling like "any
thing for a quiet life."

"Well, I've always thought, and I'm sure I'm
right," she added, confidently, "that the sky is an
immense piece of blue paper, and God has pricked it
all over with a pin, which makes the light, which
you know in heaven is very, very bright. Mamma
says there is *never* any night there, which makes the
light shine through, and those little pin-pricks we
call the stars. Then, you know, grannie," she went
on, thoughtfully, "God is very, very good and kind;

and He knew the light of the stars was not enough to guide poor sailors, like Arthur at sea; so He hung a great lamp outside the blue paper to light them on their way, and we call it the moon."

"But how do you account for the clouds, Leo?" said Mrs. Archer, unconsciously aroused to interest by the little maid's speeches. "You know the sky is not always blue; it is sometimes, nay, very often, here in England, white, and even black with thunder-clouds."

"Oh, bother," said the child, "I've not thought about the old clouds; I suppose they are something or other I shall find out presently," for she was not pleased to find a flaw in her little celestial scheme.

Mrs. Archer did not press the question; indeed she had no time to do so, for the train had reached its destination; and there was grandpapa, dear darling grandpapa, Leo's devoted slave, and untiring friend waiting for them. And then, in a very few minutes, they were all snugly packed in the carriage, and bowling along the muddy lanes and dark lonely roads towards the Grange, which had been the childhood's home of Leo's mamma. Two big cousins were at the door to receive them, the daughters of Mrs. Mildmay's brother; and then Aunt Ethel, another worshipper of Leo's, lifted her bodily through the carriage-window, so anxious was she to hug her darling once more.

Presently they were all seated round the dinner-table, so well laden with good things. Sitting up to a late dinner was a novelty and great treat to Leo; but soon a little man called "Billie Winkie," came with his little sand-bag, and threw it in her eyes, so that she could no longer keep them open. Aunt Ethel saw this, and carried her off to the great white bed, so soft and so high, in which she was to sleep with her; and very soon she was fast asleep.

Early next morning, far earlier than Leo liked, the two big cousins, Una and Ruth, came hammering at the door, calling her to make haste and come see how jolly the Grange was. So she leapt bravely out of bed, and getting Aunt Ethel to tie all the hard strings and button all the buttons out of her reach, she soon appeared "to do the Grange," as she called it. And what wonders were there, to be sure! What ducks, and geese, and chickens, and cocks and hens! What horses and pigs! and then in the fields what lots of cows and sheep! Leo was just admiring a little Kerry cow, all black without a single spot in it, when grandpapa joined them, and seeing how much she was in love with it, made her a present of it. This sent her nearly wild with delight; and when he gave her also a cock and hen with their whole brood of chickens, she could not speak to thank him, but pranced round in her joy.

Then the butler came to say breakfast was ready, and they all went in. Leo was promoted to what she liked best; at home she had always to take a plateful of porridge before she got anything else; but grandmamma would not hear of her being forced to eat what she did not fancy. I am afraid Leo's visit to the Grange was a high road to being spoiled—arn't you?

After breakfast grandpapa brought them all into his study, and gave them lots of " goodies."

" I know what I'll do with mine," exclaimed Leo, a bright thought striking her.

" What, pigeon?" said grandpapa, pinching her cheek.

" I'll make a shop, that's what I'll do; and you shall all come and buy—only you must give me real *live* money, you know!"

" And when will you open your wonderful shop, Leo?" said Una.

" This very day," she decided; "only it won't be ready till luncheon-time. I must go and make love to the cook, and see what she'll give me towards it. Is she *very* cross, grandpapa?" and she looked up archly in his face.

" I don't know anything about Mrs. Cook, darling !

but come along and we'll make love to grannie, which will be twice as good, for she has the keys of the store-rooms."

"Ah, but she can't bake my pies," said Leo, doubtfully, "and Sarah makes me such dear little ones; papa gives me sixpence each for them."

"Ah, there's grandmamma! Grannie, here's a child wants to make love to you."

"Make love to me," said the old lady, smiling. "How now little woman?"

"Why, grannie, don't you see, I want to make a shop, and I've only got these sweets in my pinny, and I want cook to give me lots more things like Sarah does at home!"

"And so she shall, birdie. Come along with me now and see what I can contribute." But the pinafore was too small to hold the treasures with which grandmamma wanted to load it; so Leo had to run back and forward with her wares many times before she said, "Is that enough, darling?"

"Oh, loads and loads enough," said Leo, gratefully. "What a dear, good grannie you are! I'll give you a kiss for it," she continued, with a naïve graciousness which Mrs. Archer thought very winning.

By half-past one the shop was ready; and by its owner proclaimed open. There were many customers that first day, for the parish priest had come in to luncheon, and the vicar's wife, Mrs. Coniston, was paying a morning visit. She had been a girl friend of Mrs. Archer's long, long ago, the difference of creed making no difference in the affection which years had failed to cool.

Everybody patronised Leo's shop; even the servants wanted to show their appreciation of it; but with a delicacy worthy an older child, she lowered her prices to suit, as *she* thought, their purses, and charged them pennies, where she had exacted sixpences and shillings from the ladies and gentlemen.

Grandpapa declared she was a " young thief," to charge so much as ninepence for a jam tart; but he gave it nevertheless; and when Miss Leo closed up her shop an hour later, she found she was richer by eight or nine shillings. There was a little fond whispering to herself as she counted over the silver and copper pieces, and a joyous smile on her rosy lips as she laid them contentedly in a corner of the drawer in which Aunt Ethel said she might put her things. And why do you think she was so happy? Just because, dear, generous little heart, all the money she had earned was to buy a new book with raised letters for " her Trottie !"

And Trottie, how was he bearing this first separation? Bravely, as he did everything; only he missed the incessant noise and teasing, and told himself he would rather be with his dear little sister, with all her rough, boyish ways, than without her, possessing the peace and quiet he now enjoyed. He was sorry he told mamma he could not write to Leo every day, for that would be teasing his mother too much; but if she would just write a tiny letter to-day he would not bother her again until Leo answered; and so, on the following morning, her young ladyship received the first letter she ever got in her life. It was addressed—

"Miss Leonora Mary Mildmay,
"Care of J. Archer, Esq., J.P.,
"The Grange,
"Barton-in-the-Clay,
"Blankshire."

As was usual with her, Leo danced round the table with sparkling eyes, unable to speak her joy, or to open her letter, but flourishing it wildly in the air, as. if to show by that how glad she was.

"Come, Leo, let me read it for you," said Aunt Ethel; let's see what Trottie says;—though perhaps it's from mamma, is it?

At this Leo looked rather indignant.

"Of course it's from Trottie," she said. "Mamma wrote the envelope, but it's from my Trottie, all the

3

same," and she handed it proudly to her young aunt to read.

"My darling Leo," it ran, "I miss you very much: but if you are quite happy with grandpapa, I don't want you to come home before you get *un*happy; but, darling, the first cross word they say, you come straight home to mother and me, and *we'll* not talk cross to you. All your dollies are quite well. I am rather glad, though, that you gave Miss Rosa to Edith to mind, for I am afraid I could not have cared her enough. Miss Violet and the baby sometimes cry, but I hush them to sleep, and then they are quite good. The old black cat died the day you went away;—perhaps it was of sorrow for you, though Sarah says she was sick for some time before. It does not seem as though you went away only yesterday; it seems as if I had not felt you near me for ever, ever so long. You'll write soon to me, Leo, won't you, and tell me if I may pluck a white rose out of your garden? I want to put it on mother's table for Our Lady's feast next week. Good-bye, from your own Trottie.

"Mother, and Edith, and Miss Williams, and all the servants, send lots and millions of love and kisses to you. Good-bye."

"Did anybody *ever* in the world have such a swee love of a brother as I have?" she asked, with glistening eyes as she took back the letter. "My Trottie, if I don't write you as long a letter as—as Aunt Ethel's plaits of hair, my name isn't Leo !"

"But who will write it for you, Leo?" said Ruth, provokingly : she was beginning to be a little bit jealous of all the petting bestowed on her young cousin.

"Oh, Aunt Ethel will;—won't you, Aunt Ethel?" and she gave her aunt one of her most bewitching smiles.

"Yes, dearie, of course I will;—to-day shall it be?"

"No, I think not, thanks; because, don't you see, I've so little to say. I'll wait until we've been to the vicarage, and round about a bit; for I could not write a letter as long as your plaits without anything to say, could I?" And then the little fairy ran off to prepare her shop.

CHAPTER III.

HE " shop " proved such a success, that Una and Ruth entertained serious thoughts of "setting up" on their own account, as a means to replenish their purses; but grandpapa declared this would be unfair, for, even if they did not take Leo's custom from her, which was scarcely likely, they would put an end to the fun which the novelty of·her scheme gave to everybody.

But Leo was a generous little soul; and no sooner did she hear that her cousins wished for a shop also, and that grandpapa had forbidden it, than she offered, with her childish graciousness, to enter into partnership with them. "It was easy," she said, "to make another sign-board, and to write 'Archer, Archer, and Mildmay,' instead of 'Leo Mildmay, Confectioner and Pastrycook,' which had been the former inscription."

The plan was adopted with great glee, but with a little shyness on the part of the big cousins, who were ashamed to find Leo more generous than themselves; and at the end of her visit, when all debts were paid and accounts squared, they found they had just eleven shillings each! Grandpapa had sent to London for the book with raised letters for Trottie; and Leo lived in daily expectation of the arrival of her treasure.

Meantime she did not forget her little brother, but stored up such scraps of child-news as she thought would please him; and then, when after about ten days' stay at the Grange, she thought she had "enough to make a letter as long as Aunt Ethel's plaits," she requested that lady to be kind enough to indite the following epistle.

" Mind, Aunt Ethel," she said, as they set about the important work, " you're not to write *one single* word of your own in it, but just everything as I say it. Trottie would not care for a letter from you; he only wants one from me."

And so Aunt Ethel began:—" My own precious Trottie,—You must not think that, because I've not written to you every day, that I've forgotten you; no, not so much as one little bit; I pray to God every night and morning to bless us both just as I used at home, and I love you just as much as ever I did, only I'm afraid I don't care so much for Harry Hill. The lady at the Vicarage, Mrs.—"

"What's her name, Aunt Ethel? Oh, there, you've been and written that, I do believe!"

"But, Leo, you told me to write everything just as you said it," remonstrated Aunt Ethel.

"Oh, but you know I didn't mean you to write that," said Leo, reproachfully. Well, go on now, at any rate.

"Mrs. Coniston has a sweet little grandson, just two years older than me. He is ever so nice. He wore a black velvet suit and blue silk necktie last Sunday; and next Sunday he is going to wear a blue sailor-suit, like your new one with the gold buttons, you know—at least, he told me so. I hope he is not a storyteller, though, for I should not like him if he was! I am sorry old puss is dead; I am sure it was because I went away, and she died of grief. Tell Sarah to get me another Kitty before I come home;—no, though! I don't think I should care for a cat; her hairs fall out on my clothes so, and stick all over me. Tell her to get a doggie or a dickie-bird instead. What do you think grandpapa gave me the other day, Trottie?—just a Kerry cow, all to myself: and a cock and hen and nineteen chickie-wickies. Aunt Ethel says there are nineteen. I hope she is not a story-teller, though, for I should not like her if she was. Una and Ruth are great big girls with black eyes that stare at you ever so hard, and great long curls, long past their waists;—oh, how I wish *my* hair was long! It's so nice to hear people say, 'See what lovely hair that child has' ('Vain little monkey,' laughed her mother, when she read this): but my poor little curls cling to my poor little head like so many hard rings! Tell Miss Williams to pray to God that I may have long hair;—she always gets what she wants—eh, Trottums!

"This is ever such a grand place! I think grandpapa must be awfully rich, he has ever such a lot of money in his pocket always; and you'll be rich, too, my own when I come home, for I've ever so much money to divide with you!

"Grandpapa and grandmamma, and Aunt Ethel, send everybody their love, and hundreds and thousands of hugs and kisses: and tell papa he need not come to fetch me, for grandpapa is going to bring me home: and we're going to stop at Manchester, that enormous big town, and buy—oh! such lots and heaps of things for everybody: I only hope I shan't spend all my money before I see you.

"Do you think this letter is as long as Aunt Ethel's plaits, Trottie?—But I forgot, you never saw her; so how can you tell? Well, *I* think it is, so good-bye, and God bless you.

"From your own loving sister,

"LEONORA MARY MILDMAY."

"There, Aunt Ethel, I think that's a splendid long letter, don't you?" she said, with a sigh of contentment, as her young aunt folded and put it into an envelope. "Don't you think Trottie will be dreadfully pleased when he gets it?"

"I am sure he will be very, very glad, Leo," returned Aunt Ethel; but, come now, it's time we got ready for that drive with Mrs. Coniston: you know she promised to take you to the sea, and we were to be at the vicarage by one o'clock, and it's now past half-past twelve. Come, hurry up," and she carried Leo off not an unwilling prisoner in her arms.

Leo had never seen the sea. This drive had been planned the very first day she met Mrs. Coniston, to let her make acquaintance with the sea, which she had never seen. You can guess her delight when she caught the first glimpse of it. She clapped her little hands with a glee which Una and Ruth, who had always lived at the seaside, could scarcely understand. And when at last they all left the waggonette to walk on the beach, her delight knew no bounds. Mark Coniston, the Vicar's little grandson, taught her how to make sand castles and to send ducks and drakes skimming over the bright shimmering wavelets, that lapped the shore with such soft-lulling noise. And then nothing would satisfy her, but she and Mark must take off their shoes and stockings to paddle about in the water. This, at first, Aunt Ethel would scarcely consent to; but Leo begged so hard, and put on such a winsome smile, that she could not resist the pleading, but let her have her way. Then there were shouts of gladness and scrambling who should be ready first. But Mark was older than Leo, and knew better how to take off his things; so he won the race, at which his little friend was a good deal put out.

Carefully, carefully he waded about, while Leo marched in with a would-be-brave air—though, truth to tell, she was mortally afraid, getting more and more so, as she got deeper and deeper. At last she found a nice smooth stone whereon to rest, where the water only came above her ankles; then, seeing another about an inch or so deeper down, as she thought, she put out her hand to steady herself on Mark's shoulder. He was going to shake her off, but unhappily for himself he was too late, for she had gripped him firmly, and before either of them knew where they were they found themselves struggling together in deep water; for the stone which Leo had thought so near had only looked so in the clear, shining water, and in reality was more than two feet below the surface. Fortunately the coachman was near, and while Aunt Ethel was screaming to them on the shore to keep quiet until help came, he had waded into the the sea, and was carrying both the children dripping wet to land, Leo loudly blaming Mark for letting her tumble, while he kept a sulky silence in his resentment against the young lady who had been the cause of his discomfiture. And so ended Leo's admiration of Mark Coniston ; from that day forward, wore he black velvet suits, or sailor's costumes, never so charming, she never said more to him than the politeness her mother had taught required.

The days had lengthened into weeks, and the weeks into nearly two months, and still Leo kept no count of the time, and never once reminded them at home to come and fetch her after her three weeks' visit was over. She was enjoying herself thoroughly, poor little mite ! Una and Ruth, the big cousins, had gone home long ago, and she reigned supreme without a rival in the hearts of her adoring grandparents and Aunt Ethel.

There had been talk of the coming "harvest home," and Leo, though not knowing what it was, begged hard to stay at the Grange until it was over. Grandpapa and grandmamma were nothing loth ; and in answer to the last longing letter, written jointly in mamma's and Trottie's names, had said that two days after the grand event they might count upon seeing their "Chatterbox."

Great were the preparations for the harvest home at the Grange, and busy with her childish and loving helpfulness were two little hands and feet, as they carried fruit from the store-closet, or ran messages for grandmamma. There was no coyness about what dress was to be worn that evening; and the clean white *piqué*, with its bows and sash of blue ribbon, quite satisfied her. Grandpapa had proposed that she should open the dance with Mark Coniston, who was resplendent that night in his black velvet suit; but Leo declined, and going over to old Staines, the butler, she asked him shyly to lead her "up the middle and down again." But Staines' legs were stiff, for he had not danced for many a long day, and so he asked Miss Leo respectfully to choose someone else. Leo, seeing a waggoner standing near, nervously twisting his fingers and thumbs, took his hand and said: "You'll dance with me, won't you, man?"

And he did dance with her, and mighty proud was he of the honour. It was a pretty sight to see the little fairy tripping along at the side of the great gawky man, who knew no more than his horse how to keep time. Before the guests, and certainly before Leo was tired of the dance, supper was announced. Grandpapa told Leo it was not usual for the ladies of the house to be present at the feast; but he had made an exception this year, because she was there; and grandmamma, Mrs. Coniston and Aunt Ethel helped to wait; while Leo looked on with delighted eyes, or tried to stuff the pockets of the mothers and children with good things.

"Have you no little boy or girl, woman?" she said, presently, to a mother whom she saw sitting alone with her husband.

"Yes, Miss Leo; only he's blind, and it worries him to come among strangers."

Poor Leo! her eyes filled with tears, and she said: "I, too, have a little brother, and he is very blind; he can't see the least thing; but I love him very, very much, and he loves me, too, and I am going home to him the day after to-morrow."

She went away to find grandmamma then, and to beg a little basket; she could not tell what it was for, she said, because it was a secret, but she was sure grandmamma would not be angry if she knew.

Then she went round and picked out the choicest sweets and cakes she could find, and, putting them neatly in the basket, she covered it with a napkin, and stealing shyly up to the side of the woman with the sad face, "See," she began, "these little things are for your poor little blind boy, say Master Trottie Mildmay sent them—don't say Miss Leo, you know— and say that the little boy who sent them is quite, quite blind, like your little son, do you hear?"

"Blessings light on your bonnie little head, and thank you kindly for remembering my poor blind

Willie, Miss Leo," exclaimed the mother, the tears gathering in her eyes while she said it.

"What a sweet little fairy it is, wife!" said the labourer, as Leo tripped away, "may Almighty God bless her, and his Holy Mother protect her!"

*　　*　　*　　*　　*

At last the harvest-home was a thing of the past— the great barn wherein the feast had been spread was empty, and the rifled dishes and disordered tables gave it such a forlorn appearance that Leo said she did not want to see it any more.

Her last day at the Grange was spent in collecting all her treasures, and of these she had become the possessor of not a few since she left home, as everybody vied in giving her all she desired. Poor grandmamma was at her wit's end to find room in the trunk for them all; and, as a last resource, had to lend her another. Of money, too, she had saved a good deal; for, unlike her usual prodigality, she had carefully put by every penny given her, so as to have it to divide equally with Trottie when she went home. Grandpapa kept this safely for her: and, after many kisses and good-byes from grandmamma and Aunt Ethel, they at last started for Manchester, where, when they reached, she was half doubtful about buying the marvellous things she

had promised to bring all the dear ones at Home.
Grandpapa, however, promising to pay all the bills,
she began to buy as hard as she knew how. He
thought she would, perhaps, buy dolls for mamma
and Edith, and a toy ship for papa; but, with a
sense beyond her years, she chose what she thought
they would be sure to like—a tea-cosy for mamma;
gloves and ribbons for Edith; the same for Miss
Williams, to whom, with all her waywardness, she
was deeply attached; a nice gold pen for papa, and
then, for Trottie, if she could but carry all the lovely
play-toy shops in Manchester on her back to him she
would be quite content. But as that was impossible,
with a little advice from grandpapa and the shop-
man, she at last found what she thought would suit
him. Then, happy as a little queen, she sat with her
head on grandpapa's knee until the train reached
Helstone and home.

There were they all at the station waiting to receive their darling back again. Mamma, holding
Trottie's hand, while a smile of heavenly sweetness
lighted up the pale pure face of the sightless little
boy. Poor little man! his martyrdom of pinches
and snubs was about to recommence; but he was
more glad than otherwise, and gave Leo, when at
last he got hold of her, such a tight hug that she
struggled and cried for mercy.

How glad everybody was to see grandpapa, too!
What wonders he had brought from Manchester,
unknown to Leo, for each one! But he could only
stay three days: grandmamma and Aunt Ethel were
lonely without him, in that great wide house, and so
he had to go. Leo gave him many hugs and kisses
at parting, and heaps of loving messages to all she
had left behind at the Grange. And so he went;
and Leo's time of holidays and petting was over, and
the old life of lessons and teasing poor patient
Trottie began again.

"Who's been doing my work all this time?" she
said, the day after grandpapa had gone.

"Oh, Mary has put the chairs round for dinner
and I've tried to run as many messages as I could for
mamma; everybody has done a little, I think," answered Trottie.

"Heigh-ho!" sighed the little woman, "I don't
think I much like work; I did nothing at all at
the Grange, and grandmamma gave me sixpence a
week; and at home mamma only gives me three
pence, and I've to earn it!"

"Oh, Leo, for shame!" exclaimed Edith; "are
you getting mercenary already?"

"I don't know what 'merceny' means, Edie;
but I know I don't like work, and you don't either,
now do you?"

"I'd a great deal rather be occupied than idle, Leo, if that is what you mean: you know the old rhyme: 'Satan finds some mischief still for idle hands to do!'"

"Silence, children," said Miss Williams, gently; "you know you must not talk in lesson time. Leo, have you learned your spelling yet?"

"Yes, Miss Williams," was the meek reply.

"Then come and say it, my dear."

But the lesson had been, as usual, imperfectly conned, and so had to be returned to be learned in play-time. Poor Leo—of all punishments this was the one she most disliked, to have her play hours shortened; but she had done wrong, and so she, like everyone else, had to pay the penalty. Notwithstanding "her dislike to work," she did the little she had to do, with the same hearty good-will she put to everything but her lessons. That night the chairs were duly put round for dinner; but there was a slight mishap which occasioned disgrace to the chair-placer.

Edith was standing in the window trying to read by the last faint minutes of twilight, and Leo, nothing thinking at the moment, removed the chair from behind her. Afterwards she saw what she did, but with a wicked little laugh, she anticipated the consequences, and for the sake of a "bit of fun," let it stay so.

As was natural, when darkness had set in, in real earnest, Edith closed her book, and thinking her chair was where she left it, she sat down, down, and when at last she came in contact with something harder than the soft-cushioned chair she expected, she heard a peal of the merriest, wickedest laughter.

"You horrible child," she exclaimed, when she had regained her feet; "how could you do such a wicked thing?"

"How could I?—oh, very easily. I only took the chair from behind you to put at your place for dinner."

"What is the matter, children?" said mamma's voice from the hall,

"Oh! mamma, you cannot think how naughty Leo's been; she took the chair from the window-seat just before she knew I was going to sit down; she deserves to be well punished, so she does; she's getting incorrigible!"

"Gently, gently, Edith dear," said mamma, "perhaps she did not do it intentionally. Did you, Leo, my child?"

Thus appealed to, Leo muttered something about not seeing it at first, but afterwards she had done it for the fun of the thing."

Mamma said she was sorry to have to punish her, but for the rest of the evening she must remain in

4

the nursery and have her dinner sent up to her there.

Delightful! thought Leo, I'd a deal sooner be up there with nurse and Fanny, and play with the new baby!

The last-named was now nearly four months old, and by everybody else was called Rupert; but to Leo, who had been very little with him, he was still " the new baby." She did not let her mamma see, however, that she thought her punishment " delightful," for then it might have been changed; so with a penitent little air, and her forefinger on her lip, she went slowly up stairs, as though she thought her exile very hard.

She had a grand evening up with nurse. Fanny, the nursery-maid, made toffee for her, and nurse told fairy-tales until tired little eyes would keep open no longer, and a golden little head nodded so unmistakably, that Fanny was fain to "nest" its little owner. Next morning, with the usual forgetfulness of childhood, she did not even remember she had been punished, and went about the household arrangements of her dolls with the usual zest, making believe to order their dinner just as she saw mamma doing every day. She found Miss Rose very poorly; so weak and infirm, indeed, that she thought a day in bed the best thing for her. So she washed and dressed her other babies, and then prepared to spend the day in watching by Miss Rosa's bedside. Trottie had been very careful of his niece's health during her mother's absence; for at the last moment Leo had decided to leave her at home. All her wounds had been carefully sewn and bandaged by Mrs. Mildmay's skilful fingers; but in Leo's delight at seeing her old favourite, all the hugs and kisses she gave her caused many a rupture, and the bran-spitting again set in.

Leo only did lessons from ten to eleven; she was young yet, papa said, and he did not want her little brain to be overburdened: so she had only one hour's martyrdom every day. At ten, then, she heard Miss Williams calling, "Leo, Leo, to lessons;" but she did not stir. "Leo, Leo, ," again came the mandate.

"Can't come," was the short reply.

"What do you mean, my dear," said Miss Williams, entering the room?

"What I say, that I can't come. Miss Rosa is very ill," she moaned, "and I dare not leave my child in this crit-critter state. Just look at her, Miss Williams;—how pale she is!"

"You mean critical state, Leo, I suppose," said the governess, scarcely suppressing a smile; "but my child I cannot let you off your lessons."

"Oh, do, please, please, dear Miss Williams," and

the tiny hand clasped her dress, and the irresistible blue eyes were raised in such earnest pleading, that she said :

"Well, well, then, for this one day; but remember, Leo, Miss Rosa must get cured by to-morrow, for I cannot let her interfere with your studies;" and she left the little watcher sitting by the doll's cradle, with a quite pitiful face.

"Nurse, do look at Miss Rosa," she murmured from time to time; "I don't think she *can* last out the day, do you ?"

"What a fuss you do make about an old doll, Miss Leo," laughed nurse; "why, the old thing's been on her last legs this year past ;—she's good for nothing but to be thrown in the dust-bin !"

At this indignity all Leo's resentment was aroused. To think that anybody could have the impertinence to say her darling was good for nothing but to be thrown out ! Words could not express her resentment, and so mightily was she offended, she crossed the room to steal some of the baby's food, which she saw on a table near the fire. Happily for her, nurse was very short-sighted; and Fanny, the nursery-maid, was not there; so she effected her theft without detection, and coming to Miss Rosa's side, she prepared to administer what she affirmed the doctor had ordered her patient. Whether it was in reality, or only Leo's imagination—to the latter *I* attach my faith—Miss Rosa gave one gasp as the spoon touched her lips, and, as her devoted mother afterwards affirmed, " gave one gentle sigh, and died."

Oh! the weeping and the wailing there was in Leo's household that day! Nurse was forthwith commissioned to make complete mourning outfits for the sisters, aunts, and cousins of the deceased doll, whilst its mother went to announce the deplorable event to its grandmamma, otherwise Mrs. Mildmay.

" You must put me in black at once, mamma; —deep, deep crape, widow's mourning, mamma; my sweet Miss Rosa is dead, and I shall never love any of my other children as I loved her!"

Mrs. Mildmay could not help laughing, and Leo became angry.

" Very well, mamma," she said, " I know what I'll do ; I'll just write straight off to grandmamma, and see if *she* won't do what I ask her. I wonder if *I* were to die, would you like grandmamma to say she would not give you black clothes?" and she turned away indignantly.

Mrs. Milmay was too amused to correct her disrespectful tone just then, and it never occurred to her again ; for in less than two hours after Leo's unsuccessful pleading, came a telegram from the Grange to say that the loving grandmamma, to whom Leo was inditing a letter with unwonted attention, was no more. She had died of heart disease early that morning. Ah! then, indeed, fell a shadow on Lincroft Villa, for everybody who had known had loved Mrs. Archer, and those who did not, felt for and sympathised with, Mrs. Milmay in her grief.

Miss Rosa's decease was forgotten, once Leo knew that grandmamma, dear darling grandmamma, was no more; and now that she had to put on black clothes in earnest, she could scarcely bear the thought that she had once wished to wear them.

Many, many days passed, during which everybody trod softly about the house, and though death had not actually visited it, every voice was hushed to a whisper, as if they felt instinctively that Mrs. Mildmay could not bear a noise.

Very good was Leo all that sad mourning time; she scarcely seemed the same child, and nurse kept constantly saying that "she had taken a leaf out of Master Trottie's book." But as soon as the edge had worn off the great, great grief, the old spirit reappeared in glimpses; and, finally, one fine morning, it asserted itself in all its imperiousness.

Mamma had been feeling lately that it was not good for her darlings to mope so much; and had reproached herself for forgetting, in her selfishness, as she called it, that they could not be expected to

feel grandmamma's death as keenly as she did. And
so she planned a delightful pic-nic to the hill-side
far away in the blue distance. The scheme was kept
a secret from everybody except papa and Miss Williams; and only on the very day, at breakfast, did
mamma unfold the beautiful prospect.

Leo jumped, and screamed, and danced with wild
delight; and Trottie smiled in a pleasant, contented
way, that gladdened his mother's heart.

"Well, away to the nursery, and get dressed,
chickens," said mamma; "for the waggonette is to
be round at half-past nine, and it's a quarter to
it now."

And off they flew. Poor nurse was at her wit's
end; for it was "nurse" here, and "nurse" there,
and "nurse, where's the brush?" and "nurse, there's
no elastic in my hat." However, everybody was
dressed in time, somehow or other. Leo, the first of
all, had everything on, but her boots were still un-
buttoned; and for some reason or other, unknown
to everybody but herself, she had left the nursery in
that state, preferring to fasten them below in the
hall. But they were contrary things, those buttons,
and would not yield to the tuggings and pullings of
the plump little fingers of their owner.

Just at that moment she espied the housemaid
crossing the hall, and she called out, imperiously:

"Come, Mary, and fasten my boots;—horrid old things, they won't button for me. Come along, and make haste, will you?"

"I'm busy, Miss Leo, now, and I can't come," answered the girl.

"But, Mary, you must do what I bid you. You're only a servant, and my mamma's your mistress; and I must go out, and I must have my boots buttoned, and you must come here and do them at once."

Was it fortunately or unfortunately that mamma was at that instant coming downstairs, and that she had overheard that ordering voice commanding the housemaid to button certain little boots?

"Leo, my child, I am very, very sorry to hear you speak to *anybody* in that voice I heard just now," she said, as she came forward. "You must stay at home; I cannot take a little girl out for pleasure who does not know how to *ask* pleasantly and politely to have her boots buttoned. Go upstairs, dear, and tell nurse you cannot go to the pic-nic."

With a grief-stricken, shame-faced countenance, Leo ascended the stairs and gave the message. Poor little Trottie! his day's pleasure was spoiled for him; for only what pleased Leo contented him. He stole softly to his mother's room, and begged hard that the culprit might be pardoned; but mamma was firm, and Leo went to no pic-nic that day.

And do you not think mamma was right, little ones? *I* do. Long years afterwards, when Trottie was a man, he remembered that day, and blessed the memory of the mother who, despite her own pain and sorrow at punishing her children, never failed to lead them in the right way.

And Leo! poor lonely Leo! she shut herself up in a room all alone, and stamped and cried herself to sleep; and when mamma came home, at seven o'clock that evening, she found her all cuddled up in a corner, having eaten nothing all day, with the golden head on a little stool, and the eyelids, heavy with much slumber, fast closed in sleep.

Gently she awoke the little sinner; and then, in that calm twilight hour, when nobody but God was there to witness it, Leo asked pardon and was forgiven. Mamma showed her how wrong it was to talk to servants so, and that if she wanted to be a *real* lady, as she often said she did, she must always be gentle and kind to her inferiors. Oh, wise, tender mother! would there were a few more like you in this weary world of ours! After that quiet twilight talk, mamma took her to the nursery for her supper; and then, as if to compensate for her loss that day, put her herself to bed. Ah! how nice that was, for mamma herself to undress her; and then, with one of mother's hands clasping hers, and the other resting on her head, while she sang the Litany of the Blessed Virgin, Leo fell fast asleep, to awake, as usual, to forgetfulness of her past misdemeanour.

———————

CHAPTER IV.

CAN you take a leap with me, little readers? If you think you can, take my hand and trust to me, and see if I do not land you safely into that day three years, when Leo lost her pic-nic for ordering Mary the housemaid. She was now ten years old, our Leo, and scarcely a bit better than before. It was her feast-day, the first of July; but, unlike other years, there was no merry-making, for papa and mamma were preparing to take Trottie to Lourdes, Mrs. Mildmay's faith hoping and praying for a miracle in favour of her child.

"But, mamma," said the little son, when first the subject had been broached, "I *know* Our Lady won't give me my sight; I feel sure of it; and so I don't think there's a bit of good in asking her."

"But, mannie," said mamma, "if you don't pray, and trust, and hope yourself, we cannot expect she will. Try and desire this thing very much, for mother's sake, won't you? For unless *you* believe and hope for your sight, our prayers will hardly be answered."

" I'll try, mamma," he replied, in a weary little voice.

And so it was settled they should go on the continent for six months or a year. But what to do with the other children! Arthur was at sea; so there need be no anxiety about him. But Edith, and Leo, and Rupert, the baby! Aunt Ethel was too young to come and keep house during Mrs. Mildmay's absence; and Edith, though she managed very well under mamma's supervision, was scarcely fit to set up on her own account just yet. What *was* to be done? Papa proposed asking his sister, " Aunt Cattie," and Leo's especial horror, to come and settle the matter; but that young lady vociferated so loudly, and declared she would surely run away if they attempted such a plan, that it was abandoned in despair.

Just as Mr. and Mrs. Mildmay were deciding it was best for only one of them to go, the mother of Miss Williams became so ill that the young governess was obliged to go home and nurse her. Now, indeed, they were in a dilemma, for it was impossible to trust things to an entire stranger, both as to the management of the house and teaching the children.

Then it was a bright thought came to mamma,

just as such generally do come when we are most cast down. Mrs. Mildmay was in the habit of going every year on Retreat to the Convent of Saint Thomas. Why not leave Edith and Leo there at school while she was away? But then there was the baby!—the nuns could scarcely be asked to take charge of *him*, though he *was* nearly four years old!

"Oh, let him go to Aunt Cattie," said Mrs. Mildmay, in despair, "she is as good as can be; it's only Leo's nonsense that makes her out such an ogress."

And so Rupert was left with Aunt Cattie, but not without dear, good old nurse to take care of him; and Edith and Leo were made ready to go to the convent.

It was a sad, sad day, that second of July, there were so many good-byes to be said; first to all the friends and acquaintances in Helstone; then to all the servants and familiar faces and things that made life so pleasant; and last of all, as the carriage turned the corner of the road, on its way to the station, and dear Lincroft Villa went out of sight, Leo indeed felt as old as if the glad old life was really slipping away from her. She cried herself to sleep on mamma's lap during the long journey Londonwards; and when papa called, "Come, Leo, here we are in sweet, smoky London," she could scarcely believe that she was really in the great city she had so often longed to see.

Then there was the hotel dinner—quite a novelty
to the children, except Edith, who was a little more
travelled than the others;—but before it was half over,
Leo was asleep again, and had to be carried in that
state to her nest. Poor, weary, little woman! sleep
on, and forget you must so soon part from mother!
A year is a long separation for you, who have only
once before left her side, and that to go to grandmamma, who loved you so dearly. Now you are going
to strangers—but strangers who will not long be
such, for they are mothers with golden hearts, full of
love for the children who are sent to them!

The morrow was spent in sight-seeing. At first
Mrs. Mildmay demurred, thinking it would pain
Trottie to hear Leo's shrieks of delight at all she be-
held. But Trottie, unselfish and patient as ever,
asked of his own accord that Edie and darling Leo
should be taken to see all the pretty things in
London.

"I am afraid that would be scarcely possible,
mannie," smiled his mother, "if we are to start for
Paris on Saturday. However, they shall spend to-
day, Thursday, in going about; and then, to-morrow,
they must go to the convent, as I promised the
mothers."

And so Madame Tussaud's, the Polytechnic, and
the Crystal Palace were each visited in turn. For

more there was not time; and tired and sleepy once more, Leo was fain to seek her cot in the great London hotel. Friday morning woke up wonderfully bright and cheery for London; so sunny was it that Leo said it was "unkind of the weather to laugh at her misery." But mamma petted and kissed her, and after a bit she felt resigned, and almost happy in the prospect of school life. She began wondering what it would all be like. Whether the nuns would be *very* cross; and if mamma was quite sure she should get enough to eat. To all of which questions Mrs. Mildmay gave satisfactory answers, which chased the doubtful look from the bonnie childish face.

The holidays were about to begin at Saint Thomas'; indeed, in less than a fortnight all the children would be scattered to their different homes. But Mrs. Mildmay begged that an exception might be made in her favour, considering the circumstances; and the nuns, ever ready to put themselves aside for others, had gladly undertaken the charge of Edith and Leo, even during the long midsummer vacation.

As the cab drove up to the convent door, Leo's heart failed her a little, and a frightened look came into those eyes which had never seen a nun of that Order before. But the sweet welcoming smile of the mother who opened the door reassured her, and holding Trottie tightly by one hand (*she* always had the privilege of leading him) and mamma by the other, she walked bravely up the cloisters into the beautifully waxed oak parlour where they were to wait for Reverend Mother.

Presently, in what seemed a very few minutes, a sweet-faced, smiling nun came into the room, and begged Mrs. Mildmay to excuse Rev. Mother, as she was "suffering much to-day."

"I'm so sorry I cannot see her," said Mrs. Mildmay, "and yet more grieved that she continues so poorly. We must pray for her very much at Lourdes, must we not, Trottie, darling?" she continued, drawhim closer. "I wanted to have shown my little boy to her so much, Mother Carlyle, but that must be when we come back, and Our Lady shall have done wonders for him;—eh, Trottie?"

Trottie shook his head, sadly, and Mother Carlyle in her inmost heart misdoubted if any good would come of the journey undertaken, as it was against the little fellow's hope.

"This is Leo," said Mother Carlyle, who was Mistress-General. "We are going to be great friends, are we not? Have you made your First Communion yet, dear?

"No, Mother; but mamma has promised, if I am *very, very* good, that Trottie and I shall make it next feast of the Immaculate Conception; only I'm afraid I shall never, never catch up with Trot in goodness," she ended, in a doubtful little voice.

"O Leo!" exclaimed her little brother, while mamma put in—"But you know that arrangement was for home, darling;—you must do here just as Reverend Mother and Mother Carlyle think best."

"And we'll hope there will be no obstacle to its taking place, just as she wishes it," answered Mother Carlyle, patting Leo's cheek.

"Ah, not *just* as I wish it; for if I make it here, and next December, too, it will be without my Trottie," and she put her arms round his neck, and hugged him, while her big blue eyes filled with tears.

"Never mind, darling Leo," consoled her little brother; "we'll pray ever so hard for each other, shan't we?—and after all, it's Jesus' will, and that is always sweet and pleasant!"

The little group had been silent during this loving conversation, and if Mother Carlyle's thoughts could have been read, I think they would have been much to this purpose: "There's material that will make a fine woman in that child; such tender love for her little brother is fit foundation for strong and lasting devotion. And as for the boy, he is our

Blessed Mother's own child—that can easily be seen."

Her little reverie was interrupted by Mrs. Mildmay asking how Reverend Mother's illness began.

"Oh," answered Madame Carlyle, "she was, as ever, working for others without a thought of self. Somebody had come to beg altar-linen for a very poor church, and Reverend Mother, finding no one free, went to fetch it herself. It was on the high shelf of a press, and in reaching up she leaned too far forward, and the wardrobe came down upon her side. Since then she has been obliged to use crutches, or be wheeled about in a bath-chair."

"It's a wonder she was not killed on the spot," said Mrs. Mildmay.

"Yes, indeed, it was; and with it all, she is *so* patient, and so thoughtful for others, and does her work with the same vigour as ever. She herself is really a miracle !"

"Mother," said Trottie to Madame Carlyle, "may we go out in the garden for a bit ? Leo wants to see it, it's so much bigger than the one at home ;—but she says it does not look half as big as grandpapa's."

"Surely, my little man ;—stay, I'll send for one of the elder children to take you round;" and going to the door, the nun called someone who happened to be passing, and asked them to send Clare Mayfield, the first medallion, to her.

Soon the young girl appeared, a tall, delicate-looking child, and hearing what Mother Carlyle wanted, she was delighted to show the dear convent grounds she loved so well to her new companions.

Trottie instinctively took her hand;—she did not know he was blind, and so was a little surprised until Edith excused him, saying:

" Our little brother cannot see, and it makes him more dependent on others."

But Leo flew to snatch her chargeling from a stranger's hand, saying :

"Thank you, but Trottie always leans on me;—come, darling, take my hand."

But Trottie for the nonce preferred Clare's, and said :

" You're a child of Mary, aren't you, Miss What's-your-name ?"

" Clare," interrupted the child. " Yes, I *am* a child of Mary."

" Then, Leo, let me hold her hand as well as yours, for I like to be near anyone who belongs to the Blessed Virgin. You're not vexed, are you, darling ?" he added, squeezing her hand.

" Oh, not an atom," said Leo, though in reality she was just the least bit jealous ; but it soon passed away when they reached the pond, or the lake, as the children proudly called it, and saw the stately swans sailing about on the bright waters; or the ducks and and drakes dabbling and grubbing for worms at its edge.

"What's your other name, Clare?" asked Leo, peering up into the first medallion's face. She was very small for her age, was our Leo, and scarcely looked more than seven or eight, instead of ten, as she really was.

"*My* name?" said Clare, waking up out of a thoughtful mood in which she had been contemplating Trottie; "oh, I am Clare Mayfield."

"How funny," laughed Trottie, "all of us here belong to the month of May, for *our* surname is Mildmay; and so we belong more than the others to Our Lady, of course; because her's is the month of May," he added, reverting everything, as he usually did, to the Blessed Virgin.

"Come, till I show you the Black Alley, Leo," said Clare, "it's quite close."

"The Black what?" questioned Leo, opening her eyes.

"The Black Alley;—come along."

"Oh, no, thanks, I don't think I'd care to see that!"

"There's nothing to be frightened about in it; its only a dark passage from the garden to the orchard, which is on the other side of the road."

"Oh, no, thanks, we'll do very well here. Come, Trot, let's sit here on the bank a bit," and forthwith she seated herself.

"You are feeling the separation, I fear," said Clare, kindly turning to Edith and placing her arm within hers, "but it won't be for long; you will be very happy here, as we all are; nobody can help being happy at St. Thomas', the mothers are all so good."

"Yes, I daresay I shall be all right after a while; but it's the first time any of us, except Arthur, have been away from mamma longer than a month; and the thought of a year's being without her frightens me," answered Edith, with a half sob.

"Perhaps it will not be so long as you think. Would you like to come into the house now;—you can, if you care to, you know?"

"Yes, please, I think I should;—only we cannot leave Leo and Trottie here alone; and I'm afraid Leo will not care to leave the swans."

"Oh, she'll be a good child and come with us, won't you, Leo?" and Clare gently raised her from the ground, and led her on to the house, talking so pleasantly the while that the swans were quite forgotten.

"No wonder this child is first medallion," thought Edith, "she's so good and gentle. I wonder shall

I ever be blue ribbon or child of Mary;—I hope so, for it would so please papa and mamma," and then she found herself seated by her mother's side.

At last the time for parting came, and the good-byes *had* to be said. Mrs. Mildmay had kept up wonderfully well until then, for the children's sake; but when Leo clung to her dress, and Edith hugged her so hard and so silently, trying her best to be brave and not cry, the mother could restrain her tears no longer, and they fell plentifully on the two sunny heads beneath her.

"You must excuse me, Mother," she was about to say to Madame Carlyle; but the Mistress-General, with the tact and delicacy of a true religious, had left the room, so that no stranger might witness the anguish of those last moments.

"You'll write often to us, mother, won't you?" said Edith.

"And you'll bring us lots of things from France, won't you?" cried the mercenary Leo. "And, papa, you've not given us any money!"

"My darling, I've told Mother Carlyle that Edith is to have half-a-crown a week, for pocket-money, and you a shilling regularly, and more if you require it;—and see, I've made ready these purses for you both!"

Leo wanted to grasp Edith's, but papa was quicker than she, and so the right one fell to her lot.

" Canario !" she cried, dancing round the room, and forgetting her grief in the joy of finding so much money in her purse. " Canario " was a favourite expression she had learnt from an old Spanish pedlar who came sometimes to Lincroft Villa; it meant nothing more than " Canary."

Then Trottie came and put his loving little arms round her neck, and with that the well-spring of her téars was loosened, and she burst forth in mingled sounds of weeping and entreaty to be taken to Lourdes.

" My precious child, it cannot be," said her mother; " try, my darling, for my sake, for Trottie's, and above all, for our dear Lord's, to bear this little cross patiently and bravely, like my own bright Leo. See, give me and papa a big kiss and hug like you always do, and then we will go so quickly you won't feel it so much ;—it will be just like having a bad tooth drawn," and with that Mrs. Mildmay kissed her and hurried from the parlour. One more embrace from Trottie, and the parting was over ;—but not its effects, and for many a night our poor little woman cried herself to sleep, thinking over the weary time she must pass before she saw mamma or Trottie again.

The novelty of the next few weeks wore much of the edge of her sorrow : the anxiety of the older children as to the result of the compositions and examinations, the preparations being made for the prize-day, and the writing of the *scrutins* for the ribbons, were all so many things to distract her thoughts.

But when the children were gone, and only she and Edith, and two others from Ireland were left, the loneliness for mother returned, and she wrote piteous little letters entreating her to hurry back to her poor, miserable Leo.

But mamma could not come; she was already on her way to Lourdes, only stopping at Bordeaux and Pau for a few days, to see some friends there. Then came the anxious time ; then, indeed, the prayers and novenas to Our Lady were redoubled with intensest fervour ; then, too, Trottie began to hope—at least his mother thought so. But no ; Trottie was only glad to be where his Heavenly Mother had once appeared. He loved to hear the story of Bernadotte, and never tired while Mrs. Mildmay or his father repeated it.

A general novena was to be offered, in which many religious communities and friends had promised to join. It was to begin on the 6th of August, so as to end for the feast of the Assumption, and then Trottie was to be placed in the miraculous Grotto, to see what Our Lady would do for him.

At last the day arrived, and with it many letters of expectant hope for Mrs. Mildmay. The father entered the Cava with the poor sightless little boy, while his mother, who could not summon courage to accompany them, waited outside in sickening dread and suspense. Long they waited, and long Trottie remained kneeling there, sightless as ever, only acquiescing to his parents' wishes, not seconding them. Far into the afternoon they waited, hoping on, hoping ever, but still the desired answer to their prayers did not come, and Mr. Mildmay was fain to steal softly to his wife's side, and breathe to her that her hopes would not be fulfilled. Then he went back to bring Trottie to her, leaving her a few minutes to take in the truth.

"I knew She would not give me my sight, papa," said Trottie, as they left the Grotto; because if she did I might grow to love the things I should see with my eyes better than Her, and She would not like that, nor should I. Don't cry mother—dear, dear mother," he murmured, as putting his hands to Mrs Mildmay's face he felt the tears there. "I am very, very happy as I am, and rich, too," he added, "while I've you, and papa, and Leo. Poor darling, I don't think *she'll* be very sorry to hear I've not got my

sight, she always loved me so to lean on her; and I
don't think it teased her."

"You were never teasing, my own," cried his
mother, in a tone of anguish. "Come, let us say
one little prayer before we return to the hotel. God's
holy will is best; He knows what is good for you, and
He is doing it, though we cannot see his reasons."

And as they knelt there, all Trottie's prayer was
that the blow of disappointment might be softened
to his mother, and those who were so anxious he
might have the gift of sight.

They were remaining some little time at Lourdes,
charmed with the beauties of the spot, when one day
Mrs. Mildmay exclaimed, with a feverish anxiety,
which, though she had striven against, she had not
been able to conquer.

"Let us go to Zaragoza, Arthur; they say there's a
miraculous image of Our Lady there;—why not try?"

"My dear," urged her husband, "if Our Lady does
not cure our poor little son in one place, I scarcely
think it likely she will do so in another."

"Never mind, Arthur, we can but try," said Mrs.
Mildmay, persistently.

And so to please her, they went. But it was the
same at Zaragoza as it had been at Lourdes: the
Blessed Virgin was deaf, or seemed to them in their
shortsightedness to be so, to their cries.

Then, when all hope had to be relinquished, and the sweet spring time had come round, Mrs. Mildmay gave Trottie his long-promised visit to Rome. The little fellow after that longed to get home to England, to tell Leo how good and kind the Holy Father had been to him, and to give her the little silver medal which his Holiness himself had sent her.

One brief visit to Loreto and the " leaning tower of Pisa," and then the long homeward journey began;—homewards in more ways than one.

    *   *   *   *   *

And Leo? How long we have left her in her loneliness! but we will go back to her, and if in following her we can do so, we will comfort her.

The long midsummer holidays passed very quietly and peacefully, the only break in them being the retreat for ladies; and that afforded very little variety to the children. True, many of the ladies knew their mother, and after the retreat talked pleasantly and hopefully about Trottie; but, then, they went away, and the days and weeks glided on till the 8th of September, when all the children returned. *That* was a noisy welcoming day ! Such new friends had to be made, with whom they had not had time to make acquaintance before the vacation; and such home stories to be told of wonderful things done in the holidays by the seaside, and down in the sweet hay-scented country.

After supper, very little of which was eaten by anyone, each division was formed, and then its mistress began telling delightful stories. In Leo's *cours* the mother was elderly, and, to the children's joy, told them about the time when she was a little girl like them, and of all the naughty things she had done. And Edith heard how *Felix*, the great Parisian confectioner, rose from being a little street cake-seller to be the emperor's pastry-cook! Then the great clock in the tower rang out a quarter past eight, and the whole school filed into St. Madeline's, where Mother Carlyle was waiting for night prayers.

These over, each mother took her own little flock up to the dormitory, and in less than ten minutes, Leo was fast asleep, dreaming about how nice it was to be at school in the convent, about mamma and Trottie, and Mother Alton's naughtiness when a little girl.

In the morning she woke up to an entirely new life, for the routine which she had been excused for the fortnight before the holidays had to be implicitly followed now. Lessons, ever her detestation, had to be perfectly learned, and promises made to mamma before leaving England had to be faithfully kept.

Poor, wee woman! her brain felt nearly bewildered with the weight of responsibility that rested, as she thought, upon her. How should she, how could she ever be good without mamma and Trottie to help her? and in her dilemma she did just about the best thing she could have done: she knelt down first, and asked our heavenly Mother's assistance, and then going to dear, good Mother Carlyle, she told her in her simple childlike way her little trouble.

Mother Carlyle comforted the little mourner, and in doing so prepared her to hear that Trottie's sight had been refused him. The nun thought she would have grieved more about it; but Leo had never been anxious for Trottie to go to Lourdes, and so the disappointment did not weigh heavily with her. With Edith, however, it was different; she had ardently wished to see Trottie, her dear little brother, like other boys, and the news grieved her sadly; but mamma's reassuring letter—for unselfish as ever, Mrs. Mildmay hid her own disappointment—consoled her a little, and by degrees she became more resigned as she grew more accustomed to the thought that her hopes for Trottie's sight were not to be fulfilled.

CHAPTER V.

THOUGH Leo had behaved herself very fairly
during the vacation, the reopening of the
school, and the consequent contact of so
many more children than she had ever been accustomed to, made her true colours appear. Mother
Carlyle was in noways surprised, for she had a wonderful insight into character, and she had known
Leo's from the very first. Indeed, now she began
to doubt whether her hopes for First Communion
could be realised, and whether she could possibly
make it on the 8th of December. But an event occurred which finally decided the matter. One day,
it was a dull afternoon in early November, and the
third division were at sewing lesson in St. Lucy's.
Leo was holding an animated conversation with her
neighbour in whispers, helped out by pantomime.
Although her little chat was harmless, it was the
time for silence, and the mistress had warned her
more than once, to each of which admonitions she
had answered glibly : "Oh, mother, I forgot."

But I am afraid she forgot only because she wanted to do so; and that, if she had been so minded she need not have forgotten. There was a tinge in Leo's character which those who loved her foolishly called determination, and which those who loved her truly (and her mamma and the mothers were among the latter) called stubbornness. So when sewing lesson was over, Leo dawdled behind, folding her work more carefully than usual, and giving it sundry unnecessary pats, which added to its dirt, but not to its smoothness.

One by one the children filed out into the passage to form the *rangement* for recreation; and the nun, seeing Leo still occupied with her workbox, said:

"Come, Leo, make haste, my child; the others have done long ago."

"Yes, mother," was the answer; "I shall be ready directly." And still she seemed no nearer the completion of her arrangements.

"Come, Leo," said the mistress, presently; "you are keeping me waiting. Make haste to the *rangement.*

Deliberately Leo put down her work, went and closed the door leading to the passage, then the other which opened on a class-room, and going up to the astonished mistress, said in the impertinent tone which had often grieved her mother:

" Now, mother, you shan't get out until you promise not to tell at *conférence* that I talked so much at
sewing to-day !''

Silly Leo ! She was like the ostrich putting its
head in the sand, and thinking nobody could see it.
If she had talked without ceasing the whole sewing
lesson, what she was now doing would only make it
worse.

But the mothers of St. Thomas' are not easily
puzzled in managing children ; and Madame Oakley,
without seeming to notice Leo, took up her basket
and walked towards the door. But Leo was swift,
and setting her back against it, she glared defiantly
at the mistress, who, in no way put out, tried the
other door.

Again Leo ran and prevented her getting out, this
time declaring that " go out she should not until she
had promised."

" Very well, then, Leo," said Madame Oakley,
sitting down, " we both remain here until somebody
fetches us, for I am not going to play hide-and-seek
with you, neither am I going to make any promise
of what I shall or shall not do."

Scarcely had she finished when the door over which
Leo was keeping guard was pushed open, nearly
introducing her nose to the floor, which she richly
deserved, and there stood—Mother Carlyle ! Leo hid

her burning face between her hands; for she *was* ashamed, while Madame Oakley briefly explained the ituation.

"Oh, come," said Mother Carlyle, kindly, not willing to use severe measures; "this is only a little fit of naughtiness. Leo, my child, you forget yourself; come now, tell Madame Oakley you are sorry, and don't be foolish again."

But Leo, not yet arrived at real sorrow, stood stubbornly silent, with pouting lips and clasped hands, and eyes resolutely fixed on the ground.

"Why, Leo, you're not yourself to-day," went on Mother Carlyle. "Do you forget your First Communion? And for the sake of gratifying your silly pride, will you forego the happiness of making it with your little brother? O Leo! how sorry *he* would be to know you were like this;—doesn't the thought of him, above all at such a time as this, make you feel sorry?

Still no answer, only the same stubborn silence, the same determination not to give in; and grieved and disappointed Mother Carlyle was obliged to resort to punishment.

So Leo was sentenced to separation until she should apologise, and gain her mistress's pardon.

Thus she was kept alone, unless when the first medallion fetched her to the refectory and the chapel.

Clare Mayfield begged her to ask pardon at once. Every persuasion she knew of she tried, but each and all were alike useless. Leo was stubborn, until at last, weary of her confinement, she sought forgiveness in an unsatisfactory kind of way, which did not promise well for the future; and it was tacitly understood that her First Communion had been indefinitely postponed.

Just then a glad message came from the Mother House in France. Four days after the feast of the Immaculate Conception would be the centenary of Madame B——'s birth, and a general holiday, or "*congé sans cloches*," was to be given, by Reverend Mother General's wishes, in every convent of the Order throughout the world. The memory of the Holy Foundress was venerated very much by the children of Rilsby, and it was a powerful incentive to their improvement to show themselves worthy children of "Mère B——." Her love and leniency to the very naughty ones sometimes gave Leo courage to "turn over a new leaf" in the rare moments when a spirit of compunction came over her, and the thought of "Madame B——'s Julia," of whom her mamma had often told her, inspired her with confidence to "begin again."

In the midst of her loving preparations for her children's pleasure, Mother Carlyle's thoughts were busy elsewhere, and the result of her musings was a general novena to be offered in honour of the Venerable Mother Foundress for Reverend Mother's recovery. It was to end on the grand holiday; so on the third of December they began, with one accord, those eighty children, to pray for her whom they loved, and with reason, so dearly.

Many were the voluntary sacrifices made by them for this intention—many the fervent prayers offered that Reverend Mother might be among them all once more;—even Leo had denied herself in many a childish way unknown to anyone but herself and God.

It scarcely seemed, however, that their prayers would be heard; for Reverend Mother's sufferings had been very acute all the past week, and on the Feast itself, as the lay-sister was arranging her room for Holy Communion, she said, gently :

"Sister, will you put my crutches on the bed; I should like our Lord to see them when He comes."

And the Sister hastened to obey. She left her then, and presently the chaplain came, bringing her hidden Lord. Once more she was alone, but alone with Him, and He was pleased to hear the prayers of so many innocent and loving hearts for his servant.

Acting on some secret—impulse it can scarcely be

called, for she never acted on impulse, but some irresistible feeling, she rose, dressed herself without fatigue, and walked steadily and firmly—the first steps she had taken for nearly a year—into the tribune above the chapel. Nobody saw her but one young choir nun, and she was so amazed she could only silently stare at her ; but Reverend Mother, in her own gentle, quiet way, asked her to thank God, and to tell nobody until later on.

When the joyful news thrilled through the hearts of the community, the double favour vouchsafed brought joy too deep for words—their Mother Foundress honoured by our dearest Lord as they had asked, their dear Superior raised up from her helplessness to her old vigour—silence and beaming faces seemed all they were equal to. But the glad uproar of the children, who felt, as children, less deeply, but more demonstratively, should not be checked ; for their joy was a tribute of thanksgiving to the dear Lord whom they had so earnestly peti- tioned for this favour, and *He* knew and liked the ways of the little ones, whom He always " suffers to come unto Him." So all joined merrily in the holiday, and Leo shared fully in the happiness of the day. She was really glad to see Reverend Mother restored to health and strength, and very proud of Edith, who, three days previously, had received the blue ribbon and her "angel's medal," and who now had begun the severer struggle to be admitted into the congregation of the children of Mary.

The Christmas holidays came and went. Short ones they were, but every day enlivened by some new pleasure which the mothers devised for the twenty or thirty children remaining in the convent.

Of course the Mildmays stayed. But they hoped for mamma and papa before long; for Trottie was now at Rome, and mother had written they would soon be home now; so Leo waited anxiously for the joyful day. But, sad to say, the efforts she had made for the late novena were now relaxed; from fairly good she became very middling, and from middling, troublesome. Mother Carlyle was perplexed to know what to do with her. Not that she committed very grave faults; but she was wild and giddy, and often lost her temper.

Trottie, however, was coming home, and poor Edith was hoping for great things in the way of improvement from his influence; for although she would never acknowledge it, he *had* an influence over her she could never resist. The sad, tearful way in which he used to implore her not to wound the Sacred Hearts of Jesus and Mary would have moved a much harder heart than our poor little sinner's.

And she, too, was glad he was coming, for more reasons than that she might tease him.

Mamma had said they intended living in London when they returned, until the midsummer holidays, when, as she had promised, they might leave school if they wished; but, to everyone's surprise, Leo did *not* wish to go from the convent. She gave the Mothers a great deal of trouble, she knew; but if they would keep her, she wanted to stay; and her parents were only too glad to let her remain.

All through the services of Holy Week, Leo had her eyes fixed on Easter Sunday, for that was the day they expected Mr. and Mrs. Mildmay, after their return from Italy. But as the longest lane has a turning, so has a long week an ending; and Easter morning dawned clear and bright, wearing the prettiest of all the three hundred and sixty-five dresses in the wardrobe of the year:

The afternoon came at last; and Leo kept looking at her little gold watch, grandpapa's last birthday gift, until the great school clock struck three. Then came Sister Margaret, always glad for the children's pleasure; and to the cry, "For me, Sister; for me," she answered:

"Forty-two and Forty-six for the parlour."

Away flew Edith and Leo—the latter, of course,

first—and bursting into the *salon*, she made straight for mother's outstretched arms; and being folded there, after those nine long, long months, the tears *would* come for very joy.

Then came papa's turn; and then Trottie's, whom she almost squeezed to death, until he called for quarter.

He was the same sweet, loving little brother who had left her, not a bit soured by his disappointment, if indeed it had been one. Mother Carlyle grieved to see Mrs. Mildmay, for she knew how hard she strove to conceal her trouble from the children.

They brought great news did papa and mamma; for Aunt Ethel was going to be married next month, and they asked as a great favour for Edith and Leo to come home for the wedding.

"It was not usual to make such an exception," Mother Carlyle said; "but as Mr. and Mrs. Mildmay had been so long away, she would make it for them."

And so in the middle of May they went home to the little Kensington villa in which they were to live for the present.

It was to be a very grand wedding; and Leo delighted in all the preparations, and not least in her own bridesmaid's finery. And a pretty sight it was, that marriage: the prettiest seen for a long time in

that church, where many weddings take place every
year. But it, like everything else, was soon over;
and Edith was not sorry to get back to the convent
from the bustle and hurry, though *she* had been the
principal bridesmaid.

Then leafy June budded forth, unmarked in Leo's
calendar by any grave misdemeanour, but also innocent of any great stretch of steadiness; and in the
first days of hot July came a bad mishap, which led
to more serious consequences.

It was one of those days when everything seems
shrivelled up with the heat. Not a breath stirred
the leafy bows of the elms, not a breeze rippled the
waters of the lake. Too idle, or too overcome by
the scorching sun, to join in the recreation, Leo
stole away from her division and wandered down
towards the pond. Even though it looked so still as
to be almost a mirror, it appeared cooler than the
dry earth and parched-up grass; and without more
ado, she shrew herself body and bones, without re-
moving a single article of clothing, into its inviting
bosom.

Silly little Leo! you did not think the lake was
so deep, did you? And you forgot you could not
swim, didn't you?

Scream upon scream she uttered, until one of the

novices, hearing her, ran to the rescue. It was not difficult to fish her out, but by the time that was effected a whole band of children and nuns had come running to the spot, fearing some dreadful disaster. Mother Lynch took her in charge, and conveyed her, dripping wet, to the house. On the way she mildly remonstrated with the culprit.

"Did you fall into the lake, Leo?" she asked, "or did you throw yourself in, as I heard some of the children saying?"

"It was so terrifically hot, Mother, I was nearly roasted alive, so I just took a dip; but I did not know it was so deep."

"I hope you have not caught your death of cold," said Madame Lynch, as they reached the infirmary, delivering her over to the Sister for treatment; "I don't know what Reverend Mother and Mother Carlyle will say to you, I'm sure!"

For many days Leo had to stay in bed after this. A bad cold was the consequence of the drenching she had been pleased to give herself; and to it succeeded a nasty, teasing little cough, which settled on her chest, and which neither coaxing nor threatening could induce to bid her good-bye.

So the examinations passed without her being able to assist at them—not, I am quite sure, that she was sorry for this privation; and prize day arrived before she was able to leave the infirmary. Then, little by little, she gained strength, though still the cough remained; and this made Mrs. Mildmay doubly anxious when she came home for the holidays.

CHAPTER VI.

THEY were going to the Isle of Wight to pass the vacation; and the little Kensington villa being topsy-turvy in prospect of the "flitting," Leo, with her usual forethought, took it into her head to amuse herself a little.

Of course Trottie was to join, though passively, in her fun; and even Edith, when she heard what was going forward, volunteered as head cook.

For what? you will ask. Simply to make toffy.

Arthur, the big brother, of whom you have heard nothing up to this, was at home now from his second voyage; so that all the young members of the family, including Baby Rupert, were there to assist in the culinary arrangements.

"Two ounces of butter," read out Arthur, "hal a pound of sugar—Moses and Aaron! that'll only give each of us a bit the size of a pin's head. Hadn't you better make it four ounces of butter and a pound of sugar, Edie?"

"All right," replied Edith, nothing loth.

"A few blanched almonds," continued the sailor, "give the toffy a nice appearance, and a drop or two of lemon-juice makes it of a delicious flavour."

"But we've not got either lemons or almonds; what *shall* we do?"

"Never you mind, *I'll* provide them," said Leo, nodding her head sagely. "Just you be patient and wait, and see what the king will send you." And with this wise injunction she departed mysteriously. But, alas! not to return.

The almonds were easily obtained. Mamma just happened to be in the store-room, and of course gave her as many as she wanted. But Sarah kept the lemons in the kitchen, and Mrs. Mildmay bade her call at the top of the stairs and tell the cook to bring her one.

Now on the kitchen door was written, in Sarah's crabbed writing: "All trespassers will be persecuted"—I suppose she meant "prosecuted;"—and this notice was put up for the edification of the children, to whom the kitchen was strictly forbidden ground.

"Sarah, mamma says you're to give me a lemon, please," called Leo, as she had been directed. No answer. "Sa-a-rah, please give me a lemon!" Still no reply. "Sa-a-a-a-rah, are you de-af? can't you give me a lemon ?" This time the little foot stamped impatiently, and the golden head with its long silken curls, which had been coveted so many years, shook vexedly. Still the kitchen was silent as the grave. Down, down, down on tip-toes went Leo, for she feared being caught, and she remembered seeing a lemon on the dresser that morning when she went with mamma to order dinner. She arrived safely at her unlawful destination, and there stood the lemon, almost saying: "Take me, I'm so large and juicy." And Leo *did* take it, whether it invited her or not—at least, poor child, she intended doing so. But Sarah had left a frying-pan full of boiling fat on the dresser, and Leo, being little, could not reach the lemon without climbing on the table.

She prepared then to mount, but one curl, longer and more capricious than the rest, caught in the handle of the frying-pan, and before she knew what she was about, or could prevent it, the whole contents was pouring over her neck and shoulders.

Poor Leo! with one piercing shriek that her mother remembers to this day, she fell fainting on the floor, dragging with her the frying-pan, and scalding her lips and face most piteously. Thus they found her, two minutes later, all disfigured and unconscious.

Three different people ran for and returned with doctors; all of whom pronounced the poor little

woman in a sad way—her recovery doubtful. At
present the extent of her injuries could not be deter-
mined.

So there she lay day after day, moaning with pain
and teased by the racking cough which had returned.
Night after night passed partly in heavy sleep, partly
in feverish restlessness; still, for Leo, she was patient; for Leo, she was grateful and good.

A change seemed to have come over her, which
her mother found difficult to understand: there was
no longing to get well, no desire to run about as she
had formerly done.

Trottie never left her side except to sleep, and
then through the long night watches the little sufferer waited for the dawning, that he might be with
her again.

There was no thought of going to the Isle of
Wight now. A shadow had fallen on the house
which made everybody anxious, and forgetful of their
own pleasure.

Grandpapa came hurrying up to town as soon as
he knew of the disaster; for Leo was his favourite
grandchild, much as he loved and cherished the
others. And numberless friends either wrote or
came frequently to inquire after the invalid.

But one step on the stairs gave Leo more pleasure
than any of the others. It was that of Father Hart-

ley, the Jesuit, who never failed day by day to spend a little time by her bedside.

Somehow, from the first she had a presentiment she could not live. So, one day when Father Hartley touched upon the subject of death he found her quite prepared.

"I know I am going to die, Father," she said, while her voice trembled and the tears started to her eyes; "and I should not care to live either," she continued, with something like one of her old smiles, while she looked at her disfigured arms and neck. Then she said, more gravely: "I'm not afraid, either; but I don't think mamma knows; and I am sure she and Trottie"—here she broke down entirely, and sobs choked her voice—"Trottie will feel it very much. Father, will you tell them; for if *I* do, they will, perhaps, think me cruel, and, oh, I don't want to be; I want, if I can, to make up a little for all the worry and trouble I've given everybody, by being patient and kind these last days. You'll tell them, won't you?"

"Yes, I'll tell them, my poor child," answered Father Hartley. He did not tell *her* that everybody in the house already knew, and that they were trying to keep a brave face while their hearts were aching for her sake.

"But why, Leo, aren't you 'afraid' to die?" asked

the Father, anxious to know her grounds of confidence.

" Well, you see, Father, I've the Blessed Virgin to pray for me," she replied, thoughtfully, " Not that I've deserved her to be kind to me, for I've been often very, very naughty, and have forgotten to say my prayers, lots of times ; but, then, Trottie is so good, and I know Our Lady loves *him* very much ; and I don't think she could leave me long in purgatory, when Trottie loves me so much ;—don't you see ?"

"Yes, I see," said the Father, smiling at her childish reasoning, and yet pleased withal. "Are you in much pain now, my child ?"

"No, not too much, Father," was the patient answer; "not so much as it might be ;—and then, the thought of our Lord on the cross helps me to bear it better; I try and think that my pain is joined to his, and that, if I am patient, I shall be all the sooner with Him in heaven. Will you give me a little of that drink, please, Father ?"

Father Hartley put the glass of iced-water to her lips, and then she said :

" I'm so glad I've been dedicated to the Sacred Heart ; it's such a nice name to have—'a child of the Sacred Heart'—isn't it, Father ? I should like it to be put on my grave when I die," she added, musingly, and with strange quietness. " You won't tell anybody, Father; but while I've been lying here I've thought about many things; and, do you know, I believe Edie will be a nun," she said, in a mysterious whisper. " How nice that would be! Three of mamma's children would be entirely God's, if so; for *I* should be dead, and Trottie—well, everybody knows *he* belongs to Our Lady; and if Edie were a nun !"

Father Hartley began to fear the end was very near when she talked in such a serious way. It was not a bit like the old Leo of former days; to him she seemed a changeling, still with the pure angel face of his ancient favourite.

" I'm afraid I must go now, my child," he said, presently. " Whom shall I send to you ?"

"" Oh, plenty of people will come without being told," she smiled; " only if you should meet Trottie, send him, please. And, Father," she added, hesitatingly, " do you think, do you imagine I'm quite too wicked to—to—to make my First Communion before I die ? I should so like to," she pleaded.

" And you shall have it my dear little girl," he replied, deeply touched by her earnestness, and thinking the past weeks of pain and suffering, borne so patiently, sufficient preparation for such a holy act. Whenever you would like to have it, tell me, and we will

7

prepare your confession together ;—thus we shall help each other, shall we not ?"

. "How good you are, Father," she said, clasping her hands in her old eager way. " You won't forget to send Trottie, will you ? Good-bye."

" Good-bye, my child, and God bless and watch over you," said the priest, as he left her.

Mrs. Mildmay did not let her remain long alone, nor Trottie, either. But a visitor took the former from her side almost before she was seated; so Trottie climbed up on the bed and lay down, as Leo directed him.

It was a pretty picture, though a sad one, those two children who loved each other so dearly : one so near the grave, and the other by his affliction unable to enjoy life, unless his bright, brave nature helped him to live in the patience of hope. Leo placed the arm least disabled under his head, while he entwined both his round her neck, and thus they lay talking together.

" I wonder what will heaven be like," said Leo, presently ; " and I wonder, oh, I wonder, will it be very, very long before I get there !"

" I've often thought of the dream you had ever so long ago, Leo," said Trottie ;—" do you remember ? It was just about the time when grannie died, and you dreamt you were in heaven."

"Oh, yes," answered the child; "I recollect now, though I've never once thought of it since. There were the golden harps, and the white robes, and the jewelled crowns.—Oh! I wonder shall I have *any* stars in *my* crown," she exclaimed, suddenly, as the angel's words recurred to her. "I'm afraid not," she went on, sadly; "for I've been so very, very naughty."

"But you've been very patient since the accident, Leo," urged Trottie; "and I'm sure our Lord will not forget that; and you've always been generous and kind. But why do you talk like that?—Do you feel worse to-day?"

"No," she answered, "not worse, only tired; and —and—and—I am sorry to pain you, Trottie darling, but I must die soon. I asked Father Hartley to tell you, but somehow it slipped out unawares. Don't fret, my dear, dear little brother! you must not, you ought not to grieve; you ought to be glad to be rid of me instead, I've used you so shamefully."

"No, no, Leo!" he interrupted, scarcely able to check his sobs; "you've always been good to me; you've always been patient with me when I've been stupid and not knowing what I was doing."

"As if *that* were *your* fault," put in Leo, with a feeble attempt at her old indignant way.

"Well, you've always borne with me; you've always loved me; and, Leo—darling, darling Leo—what *shall* I do without you?" and now the delicate little frame shook with the sobs he could not suppress.

"Don't cry, mannie dear, don't cry," said Leo, soothingly. "Our Lady will comfort you: she'll know you're lonely; and if *she* forgets, which I am quite sure she won't, I'll remind her, and see if she won't send lots of angels to comfort you, and perhaps me among the number," she added, brightening and trying to smile. "Come now, cheer up, and tell me what messages you have for me to take up there; —what shall I say to grandmamma?"

"Oh, give her my best love, and tell her how sorry I am for all the times I worried her when she was on earth. And, Leo, don't think me selfish, but if you *would* tell Our Blessed Mother, that if it only were God's will, *I* should like to go too!"

"What, Trottie, go, too! and leave poor darling mamma alone;—for I do believe Edie's going to be a nun, and there's Arthur at sea; and so if *you* died, there would be no one to comfort mamma and papa but Rupert, and he's so very, very little. No, Trottie, I don't think I *could* ask the Blessed Virgin *that*—anything but *that!*"

"Very well, then, Leo," he said, with a patient

little sigh; "you always knew better than I. Wouldn't you like to sleep now, you've been talking a long while? and if you would, I'll lie here and be very quiet."

"Yes, Trottie; I think I will," she answered, drowsily. "Tell mamma to wake me, if I don't wake myself, before the sun sets : I love so to watch the gold in the west." And saying this, she fell asleep.

* * * * * *

The summer sun, shedding his bright departing rays into the sick-room, awoke the little sufferer ere long.

"Mamma, I feel very weak; I think the Blessed Virgin must be coming very soon. Please send for Father Hartley; he promised I should make my First Communion before I died," were her first words, uttered so feebly, and with such a short, catching breath, that Mrs. Mildmay at once felt their truth.

Fortunately, Father Hartley was calling below at that very moment, anxious to know of any change, as her unusual talk that afternoon had roused his fears; and hearing that the child had asked for him, he immediately passed upstairs.

"How quickly you came, Father," she gasped; " but you were always good. My confession,—I'm afraid I forget," she said, passing her hand over her eyes;—"and you promised me my First Communion."

But Father Hartley saw there would be no time before the end to fetch the Blessed Sacrament, so he prepared without delay to administer Extreme Unction; and even as he gave the last blessing, the film gathered slowly over Leo's eyes; the feet and hands grew cold, colder; drops of perspiration, the death dew, gathered on her marble brow; the lips moved, but no sound came; a sharp, convulsive spasm shook the slight form,—and bright, loving, patient little Leo was dead! He who loveth little children had gathered her to his bosom, and she had gone to expiate in another world her childish sins and shortcomings.

Her mother stood by, holding the feeble little hands, and wiping the death damp from her pale lips and temples; and when all was over, she smoothed the bright silken hair, and folded the small hands over the weary little heart that had suffered so bravely and so patiently for two long months.

Then she wept. But who can witness her grief?

Be patient, O our God! for the heart knoweth its own bitterness, and a stranger intermeddleth not therewith!

And so Leo died; and burying her they placed, as she had wished, a pure white marble cross over her grave, with the simple inscription :—

IN LOVING MEMORY

OF

"LEO,"

"A CHILD OF THE SACRED HEART."

www.ingramcontent.com/pod-product-compliance
Lightning Source LLC
Chambersburg PA
CBHW020809020726
47495CB00008B/2645